To Chris and Sarah. You two bring good things into this world.
– Eric

For my Dad.
– Kent

Kane Miller, A Division of EDC Publishing

Text copyright © Eric Ode 2016
Illustrations copyright © Kent Culotta 2016

All rights reserved.
For information contact:
Kane Miller, A Division of EDC Publishing
PO Box 470663
Tulsa, OK 74147-0663

www.kanemiller.com
www.edcpub.com
www.usbornebooksandmore.com

Library of Congress Control Number: 2015938824

Manufactured by Regent Publishing Services, Hong Kong
Printed March 2016 in ShenZhen, Guangdong, China

ISBN: 978-1-61067-400-3

3 4 5 6 7 8 9 10

Too Many Tomatoes

Written by Eric Ode
Illustrated by Kent Culotta

Kane Miller
A DIVISION OF EDC PUBLISHING

Grandfather's garden
is popping with peas.
It's buzzing with blossoms
and bumbly bees.

It's bursting with berries
and beans and potatoes
and tall, twining vines of
too many tomatoes.

Too many tomatoes!
Too many to see!
Too many for Grandpa
and Grandma and me.

A plateful, a crateful,
a grateful hooray!
This town has too many
tomatoes today!

Bursting from barrels
and buckets and pails,
over the rooftop,
and over the rails.

Red ones and yellow ones,
shiny and round,
jumbling, tumbling
over the ground.

Tomatoes on trains.
Tomatoes on tracks.
Tomatoes on tow trucks
with cars on their backs.
Tomatoes that topple
from towering vines,
crawling and sprawling
in curling designs.

Too many tomatoes!
Too many to find!
Too many above.
Too many behind.

A biscuit to butter,
a basket to borrow.
Sing me a song of
tomatoes tomorrow!

One for the teacher,

and one for the tailor.

One for the scientist.

One for the sailor.

One for the painter,

and one for the plumber.

One for the dancer,
and one for the drummer.

One for the man
at the magazine stand.

One for the girl
with the book in her hand.

One for the boy
sleeping under the tree.

One for my neighbor,

and one just for me!

Too many tomatoes!
Too many to trade!
Make way for a downtown
tomato parade!

A riddle to fiddle,
a tickle to say,
hooray for too many
tomatoes today!